You Choose Stories: Scooby-Doo
is published by Stone Arch Books,
A Capstone Imprint
1710 Roe Crest Drive
North Mankato, Minnesota 56003
www.capstonepub.com

CAPS32624

Cataloging-in-Publication Data is available on the
Library of Congress website.
ISBN: 978-1-4342-9714-3 [Library Hardcover]
ISBN: 978-1-4342-9716-7 [Paperback]
ISBN: 978-1-4965-0214-8 [eBook]

Summary: Scooby-Doo and the Mystery Inc. gang
discover a haunted house in New Orleans.

Printed in Canada
092014   008478FRS15

SCOOBY-DOO!™

THE HOUSE ON SPOOKY STREET

written by
Laurie S. Sutton

illustrated by
Scott Neely

THE MYSTERY INC. GANG!

SCOOBY-DOO

SKILLS: Loyal; super snout
BIO: This happy-go-lucky hound avoids scary situations at all costs, but he'll do anything for a Scooby Snack!

SHAGGY ROGERS

SKILLS: Lucky; healthy appetite
BIO: This laid-back dude would rather look for grub than search for clues, but he usually finds both!

FRED JONES, JR.

SKILLS: Athletic; charming
BIO: The leader and oldest member of the gang. He's a good sport—and good at them, too!

DAPHNE BLAKE

SKILLS: Brains; beauty
BIO: As a sixteen-year-old fashion queen, Daphne solves her mysteries in style.

VELMA DINKLEY

SKILLS: Clever; highly intelligent
BIO: Although she's the youngest member of Mystery Inc., Velma's an old pro at catching crooks.

← YOU CHOOSE →

SCOOBY-DOO!

The gang is stranded in front of a creepy house in New Orleans. Only YOU can help Scooby-Doo and the Mystery Inc. gang discover who's behind the haunting.

Follow the directions at the bottom of each page. The choices YOU make will change the outcome of the story. After you finish one path, go back and read the others for more Scooby-Doo adventures!

YOU CHOOSE the path to solve the mystery of...

THE HOUSE ON SPOOKY STREET

"Are we there yet?" Shaggy asks for the tenth time from the back of the Mystery Machine.

"Not yet." Velma laughs as she answers for the tenth time.

The Mystery Incorporated gang drives along the historic streets of New Orleans. They are on a mission — to find their favorite celebrity chef's famous food joint. After a day of sightseeing, Shaggy and Scooby are looking forward to gumbo, grits, and everything barbecue.

Fred drives the Mystery Machine down a street lined with old mansions and huge trees. Long ribbons of Spanish moss hang from the branches like gray rags.

Turn the page.

"Um, I think I took a wrong turn," Fred says as he looks around at the neighborhood. There isn't a restaurant in sight. "That's weird. I followed the directions the restaurant gave me on the phone."

Shaggy moans. "Now we'll never get to eat at Chef Emireel's Ragin' Cajun BBQ Palace."

Scooby whimpers sadly at missing out on the feast he and Shaggy had imagined.

"Don't worry, guys. I'll just turn around and . . ." Fred starts to say. Suddenly the Mystery Machine begins to sputter and slow.

The van comes to a stop on the side of the residential street. Fred turns the key but nothing happens. The vehicle is dead.

"Don't tell me we ran out of gas," Daphne says.

"Okay, I won't, because we didn't," Fred replies and points to the gas gauge on the van's dashboard. The arrow points to a half-full tank.

"Maybe there's something wrong with the engine," Velma suggests.

"I'll go check under the hood," Fred says and climbs out of the van.

"Like, I don't want to be stuck here. It's creepy looking." Shaggy shivers as he gazes at the shadowy mansions.

"These homes are classic examples of antebellum architecture," Velma explains. "I read all about them before we came to New Orleans."

Suddenly they hear a loud **BANG**, and the van bounces.

"Zoinks!" Shaggy squawks as his hair stands on end. He and Scooby hug each other in terror.

"Relax, guys. That was Fred closing the hood," Daphne assures her fearful friends.

"I can't find anything wrong with the engine. But the Mystery Machine is dead," Fred declares. "I guess we'll have to call for a tow truck."

Fred pulls out his cell phone, but it is as dead as the Mystery Machine. Daphne and Velma try their phones, but their devices don't work, either.

Turn the page.

"All of our phones are dead. That's just weird," Daphne declares.

"D-do you have to use the word *dead* in this spooky place?" Shaggy asks.

"We're going to have to find a landline," Fred decides. He starts walking toward the nearest mansion.

"Wait for us!" says the rest of the gang. They pile out of the van.

Fred leads the way up to the house. The trees loom over the walkway and drapes of moss hang like tattered curtains. The air is as still and unmoving as a dead man's chest.

Fred knocks on the antique wooden door. A tall, thin man opens it and stands as silent as a statue. His frown looks like it's carved in stone.

"Uh, our van broke down and our cell phones are dead. May we use your landline?" Fred gulps, intimidated by the imposing figure.

The man gestures for the kids to enter. As soon as the gang steps over the threshold, the door shuts behind them with a haunting *BOOOM*!

They enter a foyer filled with oil paintings. The stern faces of the mansion's past owners stare down at the kids. Shaggy and Scooby shiver under their fierce gaze.

"That's weird! He just disappeared," Fred says as he looks around for the man who let them into the house.

"I guess we have to find a phone by ourselves," Daphne concludes.

"Let's split up," Fred decides.

As the gang heads off in different directions, no one notices that a pair of eyes watches them from one of the portraits.

To follow Shaggy & Scooby, turn to page 12.

To follow Fred & Velma, turn to page 14.

To follow Daphne, turn to page 16.

"Scoobs and I will look for a phone in the kitchen," Shaggy announces as the gang splits up. The two pals trot off down one of the hallways leading from the foyer.

"I hope we find a snack. I'm hungry!" Shaggy says.

"Re, roo," Scooby agrees with a sigh.

"We're going to miss out on Chef Emireel's shrimp gumbo. And his shrimp stew, shrimp soup, shrimp kabobs, fried shrimp, shrimp and grits . . ." Shaggy recites.

The pair continues to dream about the celebrity chef's delicious dishes until they finally find the mansion's kitchen. Suddenly their conversation stops dead. Their jaws drop open, and their eyes expand as wide as pie plates.

"D-do you see what I see, Scoobs?" Shaggy gulps in disbelief.

"Ruh-huh," Scooby replies.

13

Shaggy and Scooby stand in the doorway to the mansion's modern kitchen. Shiny pots and pans gleam like stars in the sky. The side-by-side, double refrigerators are as large as the Mystery Machine.

"This isn't a kitchen, it's heaven!" Shaggy proclaims.

The pals forget all about finding a phone. They head straight for the fridge! The doors open to reveal enough food to feed a Southern army.

"Like, maybe I'm not going to miss going to Chef Emireel's place after all," Shaggy says and reaches for a barbecued turkey leg.

"Y'all just hold up there, boys," a strict voice commands. "What y'all doin' in mah kitchen?"

Shaggy and Scooby freeze in mid-grab. When they turn to face the owner of the voice, they gasp in surprise. A figure dressed all in white stands before them.

"R-rit's a rhost!" Scooby yelps.

If Shaggy and Scooby run away, turn to page 18.
If they stand frozen in fear, turn to page 25.

Fred and Velma head down a long hallway
to look for a phone. Velma is fascinated by the
antique architecture and furniture.

"This is like being in a museum," Velma sighs
in awe. "Just think of all the history this house
has seen."

"It looks pretty old," Fred agrees. "It also
looks a lot larger on the inside than the outside. I
mean, it seemed small from the street."

"It's probably an optical illusion, like *trompe
l'oeil* painting," Velma suggests.

Fred doesn't pay much attention to Velma as
she starts talking about painting techniques and
antebellum architecture. He is more interested in
finding a landline and getting out of the house. It
gives him the creeps.

A cold draft of air brushes against the back
of Fred's neck. It makes him shiver. He turns
around, but all he sees is an ancestor's portrait
glaring down at him. That makes him shiver even
more.

Suddenly the eyes in the portrait seem to move! Fred blinks and wonders if he just imagined seeing that.

"Maybe it was *trompe l'oeil*," Fred mutters.

Fred looks around for Velma to ask her to come look at the painting, but she has wandered out of sight. "Where's an art expert when you need one?" Fred sighs and stands on tiptoe to peer at the portrait.

Fred braces his hands on the wall on either side of the painting. Suddenly the wall pivots and opens up! Fred loses his balance and falls into the opening. The wall section swivels closed without a sound.

When Velma comes back down the hall a moment later Fred is nowhere to be seen.

"Where did Fred disappear to?" Velma wonders aloud. "I wish he had told me he wanted the two of us to split up."

Now it is up to Velma to search for a phone by herself.

To follow Fred, turn to page 21.

To follow Velma, turn to page 27.

The members of Mystery Inc. head off in different directions to look for a phone. Shaggy and Scooby gallop away in search of the kitchen. Fred and Velma pair up and leave Daphne standing by herself.

"I guess I'm on my own." Daphne shrugs.

Daphne begins to walk down a long hallway. The walls are packed with family portraits. Some of the paintings look very old. Other portraits are newer. All of the frames have nameplates to identify the person in the picture.

"Violet LaFleur, Daisy LaFleur, Rose LaFleur," Daphne reads aloud as she strolls. "Wow, the LaFleur family sure liked flower names."

One portrait in particular attracts Daphne's attention. It is a painting of a very handsome man in a Civil War uniform. Daphne looks at the nameplate.

"Michel LaBarre. Why, I do declare, you are a handsome devil!" Daphne giggles and fans herself with her hand like a Southern belle.

As Daphne turns away from the portrait and continues down the hall, she doesn't notice the glint in the eyes of the painted image.

"Hello? Is anybody in here?" Daphne asks as she knocks on one of the doors lining the hallway. She opens the door and peeks inside.

There is no phone, but the room is the perfect picture of Civil War décor. Daphne goes farther down the hall and opens another door. The room on the other side is decorated with Art Deco furniture from the 1920s, but still there is no sign of a telephone.

"Maybe the next room will be more modern and have a landline I can use to call a tow truck," Daphne hopes as she reaches out to turn the doorknob on the third door.

Suddenly Daphne hears a strange sound. She isn't sure if it's coming from down the hall or inside the room. She isn't sure what the sound is at all!

If Daphne goes down the hall to investigate, turn to page 23.
If she goes inside the room, turn to page 29.

"Ha-ha, Scoobs! That's not a ghost, that's a chef," Shaggy assures the horrified hound. "They always dress in white."

But Shaggy has a change of opinion when the figure rises into the air and screeches.

"Of course, I could be wrong about that," Shaggy admits. "Run!"

Every limb spins on the terrified twosome. Their arms and legs churn like boat propellers.

"Like, why isn't the scenery changing?" Shaggy wonders. He and Scooby seem to be going nowhere despite their speed.

"Rit's got us!" Scooby gulps. The ghost has both of them by their collars. "Re're roomed!"

"Zoinks! Put it into overdrive, Scoob!" Shaggy shouts.

The pals rev up the revolutions on their fast and furious feet. They zoom around the kitchen, dragging the startled specter with them. *BONG!* *BING! BANG!* They run into the pots and pans hanging from the ceiling rack.

At last the scary spook loses its grip on Shaggy and Scooby. It lands on the kitchen floor with a stockpot over its head. The impact makes the cooking vessel ring like Big Ben.

Shaggy and Scooby never notice. They are so terrified that they keep running. They stop only when they face a wall of food. **SCREEEEECH!** Their heels skid to a halt.

"Am I dreaming, Scoobs?" Shaggy whispers in awe at what he sees.

"If rou are, Ri am, too," Scooby slobbers.

The pals swivel their heads to gaze at shelves crammed with jars of homemade jams and jellies. Stacks of baked pies stretch to the ceiling. A rack filled with cooling pastries takes up another wall of the room.

"Like, we're in pie paradise," Shaggy sighs.

"Not for rong!" Scooby yelps. He points his paw at something behind his pal.

The chef swoops straight at them!

If Shaggy and Scooby escape the ghost, turn to page 32.
If Shaggy and Scooby get caught, turn to page 48.

Fred falls through the hidden door in the wall and tumbles into a secret passageway. Everything around him is gloomy and dusty. The only light in the spooky space comes from small holes in the wall. Fred gets to his feet and takes a closer look at the holes.

"These are the eyes in the portraits on the other side. They're spy holes!" Fred realizes.

Fred puts his eyes up to the holes. He can see Velma in the hall on the other side of the wall. She is looking around as if searching for him.

"Hey, Velma! I'm behind the wall!" Fred shouts.

Velma doesn't hear him. She shakes her head and walks away down the hall.

"Wait, Velma! I found a secret passage. It's cool," Fred calls after his friend.

Fred tries to follow Velma through the spy holes spaced along the passageway. He rushes to each pair of holes, but Velma walks too fast for him to keep up.

Turn the page.

Fred loses track of Velma. He also loses track of where the secret door is. Fred tries to find it by walking back the way he came. He presses against random places on the wall, but everything is solid.

"If I don't find a way out I could be trapped in here forever," Fred whispers.

As Fred wanders along the gloomy passageway he hears strange sounds. He recognizes some of the noises as timbers creaking or plaster falling. He's not afraid of those. What makes him nervous are the sounds he can't identify. Fred's mind starts to create monsters to match the moans and groans he hears.

"Sometimes I think that my own imagination is my worst enemy," Fred admits. "I'm beginning to scare myself!"

Suddenly the path that Fred is following splits into two. There is no way to know which branch will take him to a way out.

"I have to choose," Fred realizes.

If Fred chooses to go left, turn to page 34.
If Fred decides to go right, turn to page 52.

"Oooh, I know I should just keep looking for a phone and ignore that strange sound, but I want to know what it is," Daphne says, unable to contain her curiosity. She turns away from the door and starts to walk down the hall.

The farther down the hallway she walks, the louder the sound becomes. At last Daphne recognizes it as the chime of crystal drinking glasses clinking together. Then, she hears people laughing.

"Someone's having a party!" Daphne realizes. Excited, she hurries forward.

Daphne comes to a pair of tall, double doors. The doors are closed, but Daphne can clearly hear the sounds of people having a good time. She decides to peek inside at the festivities. Daphne opens one of the doors just a crack and puts her eye to the small opening. What she sees makes her gasp!

Turn the page.

Daphne gazes in awe at a beautiful ballroom. Ladies and gentlemen dressed in antique attire dance around the room to a waltz.

Dazzled, Daphne opens the door and goes into the room. She stands and watches the dancers, admiring the dresses and jewelry. The three-count rhythm of the waltz is almost hypnotic. A man dressed as a Confederate Army officer walks up to her, but Daphne doesn't notice him until he is right in front of her.

"Welcome. My name is Michel LaBarre," the man says with a bow. He takes Daphne's hand and kisses it. "Please join us."

The moment Michel touches her hand, Daphne is transformed. Suddenly she wears a silk gown and diamonds. Michel sweeps her onto the dance floor. As they spin, Daphne begins to feel dizzy. She wonders if she's dreaming when Michel bares vampire fangs and bends toward her neck!

"If this is a dream, I want to wake up!" Daphne moans.

If Daphne manages to wake up, turn to page 36.
If Daphne doesn't snap out of it, turn to page 55.

The ghoulish figure waves its ghostly arms at Shaggy and Scooby. The two pals stand rooted to the spot in terror. Suddenly Shaggy starts to shovel food into his mouth. The specter looks at him in confusion.

"Hey, I always eat when I'm nervous," Shaggy explains with a shrug.

In moments, the refrigerator is nearly empty and Shaggy's stomach expands like a balloon. Scooby shoves the super-size Shaggy toward the ghost. Shaggy bounces off the specter and the ghoul goes flying across the kitchen! It lands in a stack of pots and is buried under the cookware.

"*Buuuurp!*" Shaggy belches and deflates.

Scooby waves his paw in front of his nose and grimaces.

"Sorry, pal, there must have been a lot of garlic in that bowl of gumbo," Shaggy says.

BANG! CLANG! The ghost digs its way out of the mound of pans. It glares at the pals with a furious frown on its fearsome face.

Turn the page.

"Ruh-roh," Scooby gulps.

"Run!" Shaggy shouts.

The buddies take off in two different directions. The specter is left standing still, wondering which one to chase. By the time it decides to go after Shaggy, both targets are gone.

Scooby tries to hide behind a rack of chef's aprons, but his shivering makes them shake on the hooks. The ghoul grins when he sees Scooby's big feet poking out below the aprons. It tiptoes up to the heedless hound. The spook reaches toward the rack of aprons. Poor Scooby-Doo doesn't have a clue!

CLAAANG! Shaggy comes up from behind the fiend and bangs a pair of pot lids like cymbals against its head. The vibration makes the ghost resonate like a tuning fork. It wobbles away on unsteady feet.

"Let's get out of here, Scoobs. This is one kitchen I don't mind leaving!" Shaggy declares.

If Shaggy and Scooby search for the gang, turn to page 68.
If they hear Velma scream, turn to page 86.

Velma decides to search for a phone by herself. Fred has disappeared, but she's not worried. "Fred probably decided to split up and forgot to tell me," Velma concludes.

When Velma turns to walk down the hallway, she is suddenly confronted by a woman dressed in black. The stranger wears a dark veil covering her face, and Velma can't make out her features.

"Why have you entered this house?" the woman asks.

"Our van broke down, and we're looking for a phone to call a tow truck," Velma explains. "The butler let us in. At least, I think he was a butler."

"This house is not safe for strangers," the woman continues. "You should leave at once."

"Um, okay, as soon as I find a phone — and my friends," Velma agrees. Something about the woman makes her shiver.

"You have been warned," the woman says ominously and walks away.

"That was spooky," Velma says.

Turn the page.

Still wondering about the strange woman's weird warning, Velma walks down the hallway to a nearby room. When she enters the room she sees that the walls are covered with shelves and shelves full of books. Curious, Velma looks at some of the titles.

"*Modern Witchcraft, The Book of Mediums, Ghost Hunting Made Easy,*" Velma reads aloud. "Jinkies! Everything here is about the world of magic and spirits."

Velma's sharp eye notices something out of the ordinary on the bookshelf. One of the books has a title that has nothing to do with ghosts or witches.

"*Hmmm.* What's a book about baseball doing here?" Velma wonders. She reaches out to pluck the book from the shelf.

"I wouldn't do that if I were you," a voice warns from behind her.

"What?" Velma gasps as her hand hovers over the book.

If Velma pulls the book from the shelf, turn to page 71.
If Velma pulls back her hand, turn to page 89.

Daphne pauses, trying to decide if the sound she hears is coming from behind the closed door in front of her. The more she listens, the more certain she becomes. The sound seems to be someone singing, and it's coming from the other side of the door. Daphne turns the knob and opens the door. She is surprised at what she sees.

"Oh!" Daphne exclaims.

She gazes at three elderly women sitting around a table. The ladies are thin and as gray as ghosts. Their hair is wispy like cobwebs and just as pale. The sound that Daphne thought was singing is actually a chant. It's in a language Daphne doesn't recognize.

"Um, excuse me. I'm looking for a phone," Daphne says hesitantly.

The women either don't hear Daphne over their chanting or decide to ignore her. They don't respond to the presence of another person in the room.

Turn the page.

Curious, Daphne steps closer to the trio. Now she can see that they all have their hands on a large crystal ball in the center of the table. Daphne gasps at the sight of something writhing inside the globe! She also recognizes the women from the portraits out in the hall.

"You're Violet, Daisy, and Rose LaFleur!" Daphne realizes. "But . . . you're dead!"

At the mention of their names, the ladies stop chanting. They glare at Daphne with furious eyes, but their expressions turn to fear in the next second. Whatever is trapped in the crystal ball makes its escape!

A ghost swirls up out of the globe like a tornado. It whirls around the three women, and they dissolve like mist in the sun. Then the whirlwind comes toward Daphne!

If Daphne escapes the whirling wraith, turn to page 73.
If Daphne is caught, turn to page 92.

Shaggy and Scooby have their backs up against the wall in the pie pantry. The gruesome ghost floats between them and the door. It's the only way out of the room. There are no windows and no escape.

"We're doomed!" Shaggy wails.

"Re're saved!" Scooby cheers. He points to a trapdoor under their feet.

"Who knew a dog could have an eagle eye?" Shaggy says. "Come on, buddy, there's nowhere to go but down!"

The pals pull up the trapdoor just as the ghost rushes at them. ***BONK!*** The spook crashes into the hatch and staggers back. It rubs its haunted head as Shaggy and Scooby escape down the opening.

The trapdoor shuts above their heads, and the pals are plunged into darkness. The whites of each other's eyes are the only things they can see. The air is chill and Scooby can feel dirt under his paws. The damp, dark underground makes Scooby think they could be in only one place.

"Re're in a g-g-grave!" Scooby howls in horror.

Suddenly a shaft of light shines down on them from above. Scooby clutches Shaggy in a hug. "Ri don't want to go rinto the light!" he sobs.

"Um, Scoobs, that's not an angel coming for us." Shaggy points up at the pale figure glaring down at them. "It's the kitchen ghost!"

The frightening phantom starts to float down toward the terrified friends.

"Dig!" Shaggy shouts.

Scooby becomes a tunneling machine. His paws spin, and he burrows like a gopher into the ground. So does Shaggy. He imitates his canine companion and makes like a prairie dog!

Shaggy and Scooby burrow blindly until they finally break above ground. Shaggy pokes his head up out of the dirt and looks around.

"Scoobs, you're not going to like where we are," Shaggy tells his friend. "Like, even *I* don't like where we are!"

Turn to page 38.

Fred turns to the left and starts to walk down the passageway. It gets darker and darker with every step. There are no more spy holes in the wall to leak light into the narrow space. Soon Fred is forced to hold his hands against the walls just so he can feel where he's going.

"Maybe this wasn't the best choice," Fred concludes.

Fred is about to turn back when he sees a small flicker of light. He hopes it's another set of spy holes. He hurries toward the faint glow.

Suddenly Fred realizes that he has made a terrible mistake. He skids to a halt, turns around, and starts to run away from the light. The glow is not from a pair of spy holes — it's two ghostly eyeballs!

"*Yaaaa!* This direction was definitely not the best choice!" Fred shouts as his legs spin at top speed.

A horrible howl follows Fred as he flees. He glances over his shoulder and doesn't like what he sees. A spooky spirit is pursuing him through the passageway. Fred runs down the dark, narrow corridor as the ghastly ghost reaches out and tries to grab him. He feels the touch of freezing cold fingers graze the back of his neck.

"Yikes!" Fred yelps and picks up speed.

The corridor stops in a dead end but that doesn't stop Fred. **SMASH!** He crashes through the plaster wall and leaves behind a hole in the shape of his body. The ghost halts at the threshold between darkness and light. Its eyes glare as it watches its prey escape.

Turn to page 42.

"Jeepers! I had the strangest dream! I thought I was at a Civil War ball!" Daphne exclaims as she opens her eyes. A moment later she notices that she is lying on the floor and looking up at the ceiling.

Daphne gets to her feet and looks around. She is in the ballroom, just like she remembers, but there aren't any dancers or party guests. She looks down at her clothing. She is dressed in her regular clothes.

"Oh, I really liked that dream dress," Daphne sighs, disappointed.

Suddenly something sharp pokes her palm.

"*Ow!*" Daphne gasps. She opens her clenched fist and finds a small, metal object in her hand.

"This looks like an old military medal. But . . . how did I end up with it?" Daphne wonders as she holds up the pin and inspects it. She begins to get excited. "There's a mystery in this mansion, and this is a clue!"

When Daphne finds the rest of the gang she shows the medal to them. Velma turns the pin over and over in her hand as Daphne tells her friends about her dream.

"I don't think this is a military award," Velma says.

"What makes you say that, Velma?" Fred asks.

"Well, it says 'LaBarre Le Roi,' which means *LaBarre the king*," Velma replies. "I think this is a royal seal."

"That's what the man said his name was! LaBarre. Michel LaBarre," Daphne exclaims. "And I've seen his portrait in this house."

Daphne leads the gang down the hallway to a full-length, life-size portrait of a handsome gentleman dressed in a Confederate Army uniform. She takes the pin from Velma and presses it up against the medal in the painting.

Suddenly there is a sharp **CLICK** and the picture frame swings from the wall like a door. The kids peer into the darkness beyond.

Turn to page 45.

Shaggy and Scooby realize that they are in a graveyard. Moss-covered tombstones surround them. Fog creeps along the ground and creates a blanket of shifting white mist.

The frightened friends climb up out of the hole. Shaggy turns around and around, looking for an exit from the cemetery.

"Like, I can't see a way out through the fog," Shaggy moans. "We're going to be here forever."

"Oh, it ain't so bad once y'all get used to it," says a voice with a Southern accent. Shaggy and Scooby turn to see an elderly gentleman dressed in antique clothing.

"Zoinks! Where did you come from?" Shaggy yelps in surprise.

"I've been here a long time," the man replies. "You boys don't belong in the cemetery. Let me show you to the gate."

"Th-thanks, mister," Shaggy stammers.

"Call me Beauregard." The man smiles.

Shaggy and Scooby are very happy when they see the gate. They rush toward the exit but Beauregard stops them.

"Will y'all do something for me when y'all get back up to the house?" Beauregard asks.

The words he whispers in their ears make their eyes go wide. They run away from the old man as fast as their legs can carry them.

Shaggy and Scooby burst through the front door of the house. They find the rest of the gang in the foyer talking to a woman dressed in black.

"Where have you been?" Daphne asks.

"We've been talking to an old man about a ghost problem," Shaggy replies.

"Oh! Can you help my family? This house has been haunted for years," the woman pleads.

"Never fear, Mystery Inc. is here," Fred announces. "We're experts on the unexplained."

"And we know a ghost who has some explaining to do," Shaggy declares.

Turn the page.

"Reah, ret's ro!" Scooby exclaims, pointing toward the kitchen.

When they all reach the mansion's kitchen, they are confronted by the spooky spirit!

"*Yaaa!* It's the ghost!" the woman shrieks.

"Like, you mean fake ghost," Shaggy declares. Scooby sits on the ghost's chest and Shaggy pulls off its mask. A man's face glares at the gang.

"You meddling kids!" the guy grumbles.

"Uncle Buford!" the woman exclaims.

"I've been posing as a ghost to get you to abandon the house so I can be the only heir," Buford admits. "How did you know?"

"Like, the old guy in the cemetery told us," Shaggy says. "His name was Bow-regard."

"You mean Great Grandpa Beauregard?" the woman gasps. "He's been dead for a hundred years!"

THE END

To follow another path, turn to page 11.

Fred crashes out of the secret passageway and into the mansion's living room. He is running so fast that everything around him is a blur. He doesn't know where he is at first.

"Fred!" a voice yells and snaps him back to awareness.

"Velma! There you are," Fred grins as he sees his friend. "I found a secret passageway behind the wall."

"No kidding," Velma replies and points to the Fred-shaped opening in the living room wall.

"I was being chased by a ghost!" Fred explains.

Velma pokes her head into the hole in the wall and looks around inside the opening.

"I don't see any ghosts. But this passageway is cool. I want to investigate!" Velma says.

"No way!" Fred replies. "I mean, we don't know if it's safe."

"If it was safe enough for you to run around in there, it's safe enough for me," Velma decides and steps into the opening.

"Why am I doing this? I just got out of there and now I'm going back in," Fred moans as he follows Velma through the wall.

"This is great! How did you find it?" Velma asks as she looks around at the hidden passageway.

"I fell through a secret door after I saw the eyes in a painting move," Fred says. "I thought it was *trompe l'oeil*."

"Someone was watching us!" Velma declares.

"I guess so. I found spy holes in the walls." Fred shrugs.

"That's fantastic! I want to see them!" Velma exclaims. She jogs down the passageway and deeper into the dark.

"I was afraid you were going to say that," Fred groans as he follows Velma into the gloom.

Suddenly Fred hears a scream. The sound echoes against the walls of the secret passageway until it finally dies.

"Velma!" Fred shouts in alarm.

Turn the page.

Fred pushes his terror aside and runs toward the sound of Velma's voice. His friend is in danger, and he wants to save her!

"Velma!" Fred yells when he sees her lying on the ground with a ghost looming over her.

Fred tackles the gruesome ghoul. The two of them roll down the passageway like bowling balls down a bowling lane. **SMASH!** They hit the wall and come to a stop. Fred comes up with something in his hand.

"It's a mask!" Fred exclaims.

"You meddling kids! You've ruined my scheme!" the man grumbles. "I was posing as a ghost to make my cousins leave the mansion."

"I'll bet you were looking for a family treasure hidden in the secret passageways," Velma says.

"How did you know? You kids should start a detective agency," the man says.

THE END

To follow another path, turn to page 11.

"Rat's rooky," Scooby-Doo decides.

"Come on, guys, let's see where this leads," Daphne says as she steps through the secret door.

"No ray," Scooby insists and sits down.

"I'm with Scoobs," Shaggy agrees. He leans against his pal and crosses his arms.

"Would you come along for some Scooby Snacks?" Daphne asks as she pulls a box of the treats from her purse.

"Rokay!" Scooby pants.

Daphne tosses a few morsels in the air, and Scooby gobbles them down.

"Hey, what about me?" Shaggy whimpers. He holds up his hands like paws and begs.

"Here you go." Daphne laughs and gives Shaggy some Scooby Snacks.

The gang steps past the painting and into a gloomy passageway. Daphne takes a small flashlight from her purse and leads the way down a flight of stone stairs.

Turn the page.

"This doesn't look like any basement I've ever seen," Velma points out as the gang reaches the bottom step.

They walk into a small room lined with blocks of granite. The chamber is empty except for a massive stone coffin.

"Zoinks! We're in a tomb!" Shaggy screeches.

"Relax, Shaggy. It's not like the occupant is going to sit up and say hello," Fred says.

"Look!" Daphne points at the stone sarcophagus. "The royal seal is carved into the coffin!"

Daphne goes over to the coffin and presses the metal pin into the symbol etched in the stone. Suddenly the heavy lid slides back and the occupant sits up. "Hello," he says.

"*Yaaaa!*" Shaggy and Scooby scream. Their legs spin, and they zoom out of the tomb.

Fred and Velma run behind their buddies. But Daphne doesn't move. She is shocked to see that the man in the coffin is the man from her dream.

"You are more beautiful in real life than you were in my dream," the man says. "Thank you for rescuing me from my prison."

"M-Mr. LaBarre?" Daphne stammers.

"Please, call me Michel," LaBarre says.

Before Daphne can blink, he is out of the coffin and kissing her hand. He takes the metal pin from her grasp and attaches it to his lapel. LaBarre smiles and reveals vampire fangs. Daphne gasps as he bends toward her neck.

When Daphne returns to the rest of the gang, they are sitting in the Mystery Machine, which is working again.

"Am I glad to see you!" Daphne tells her friends. She smiles and reveals her new fangs.

"Ruh-roh," Scooby gulps.

"Zoinks! We're doomed!" Shaggy moans.

THE END

To follow another path, turn to page 11.

The spirit looms in the pantry door with a menacing scowl on its pale face. It shakes a ghostly rolling pin at Shaggy and Scooby-Doo.

"Zoinks! We're cornered!" Shaggy yells. The room has no windows. There's no escape.

"Re're roomed!" Scooby whimpers.

The ghost cackles an eerie chuckle and slides across the small room toward the two pals. Suddenly Shaggy holds up his hand in a gesture for the spook to stop. The horrifying phantom halts.

"Like, don't we get a last meal?" Shaggy asks.

The ghost scratches its head and shrugs.

Shaggy takes that as a "yes" and grabs a pile of pies. He chomps down on one and grins with his mouth full of blueberries.

"Delicious! This is the best pie I've ever had!" Shaggy exclaims.

"Really?" the ghost asks, smiling. "I made it myself."

"You bet! Here, you should have some," Shaggy says and pushes a whole pie in the ghoul's face.

The specter staggers away from the two pals. It bumps into a stack of flour sacks and falls. The bags break open and cover the ghost with white flour from its horrible head to its terrible toes.

"Run!" Shaggy shouts to Scooby.

The frightened friends run over the spook and out of the pantry. They look around the kitchen for a place to hide. Scooby jumps into a huge, empty soup pot. There's no room for Shaggy so he disguises himself as a string mop. He plops a bowl of cooked spaghetti on his head and stands as stiff as a rod.

Shaggy peers out from the spaghetti noodles and watches the ghost burst out of the pantry. The ghoul looks around for Scooby and Shaggy, but it doesn't see them anywhere. Shaggy almost heaves a sigh of relief, but then he realizes that the ghost isn't leaving the kitchen. Instead, the spook starts cooking!

Turn the page.

Shaggy tries not to gulp too loudly as he sees the specter chop vegetables and dump them in the pot where Scooby is hiding. Next it tosses in some herbs, Cajun spices, and pieces of chicken and sausage. Shaggy realizes that Scooby is about to become the secret ingredient for a special Southern gumbo!

"*Nooo!* Scooby-Doo, I'll save you!" Shaggy shouts and abandons his disguise.

The ghost is startled by Shaggy's sudden appearance. So is Scooby. He pokes his head up out of the pot, snacking on some okra and shrimp.

"*Mmmm*, rastey," Scooby declares.

"Run, Scoob, or you're going to be what's for dinner!" Shaggy warns his pal.

As soon as Scooby-Doo realizes where he is, he leaps straight up and out of the pot. He collides with the pot rack above his head. *CLANG! BANG!* Suddenly Scooby is wearing the cookware!

Turn to page 58.

"*Hmmm.* I guess I have a fifty-fifty chance of finding a way out of here no matter which direction I go." Fred shrugs and turns to go down the path on the right.

The hallway gets darker and gloomier with every step Fred takes. Soon it is almost impossible to see where he is going. There is a faint rectangle of light in the distance and Fred heads toward it.

"I sure hope that's a way out of this place," Fred says. "I don't want to be stuck in here forever."

When Fred reaches the spot, he is relieved to see that it is a door. He's at the bottom of a staircase, and the light is coming from the top of the stairs. Suddenly he sees a human-shaped shadow move at the top of the stairs.

"Hey! Hello!" Fred shouts. "How do I get out of here?"

Fred runs up the staircase, but no one is there when he gets to the top. Fred scratches his head in confusion.

"I'm sure I saw somebody," Fred says. "Hello! Is anybody here?"

Suddenly Fred hears a strange sound. At first he thinks it's a moan. Then he realizes that it's someone calling his name.

"*Freeed . . . Freeed!*" the distant voice wails.

A chill goes down Fred's spine. The voice doesn't sound human to him!

"That sure sounds spooky. Maybe I'll keep looking for a way out on my own," Fred decides.

Fred starts to walk down the passageway, but as he moves ahead the voice gets closer! Fred doesn't want to go back the way he came. He knows there's no way out back in that direction. He has to go forward. "Fred!" the voice shouts from behind him.

"Yikes!" Fred shrieks and jumps almost to the ceiling.

Turn the page.

"Fred! It's me!" Daphne says. "I heard you call out and was trying to find you. I'm lost!"

"What do you know, that makes two of us," Fred confesses.

"Oh, no! I was hoping you knew a way out of here," Daphne groans.

"I've been looking, but so far no luck," Fred says.

"Well, maybe we'll have better luck if we work together," Daphne suggests.

"Okay," Fred agrees. "I've got a plan. Don't split up!"

The two friends start to walk down the passageway. They don't get far. Suddenly they hear a spooky noise. Daphne gulps in fear. But Fred isn't afraid.

"It's probably the gang looking for us," Fred concludes. "Hello! Here we are, guys!"

But it's not their friends who find them!

Turn to page 62.

"Daphne, are you in here? We found a phone," Fred calls out as he and the rest of the Mystery Inc. gang come into the ballroom.

They find her, all right. She is lying on the floor, unconscious.

"Daphne!" Fred shouts and runs to her side. "What happened? What's the matter?"

"Like, why would Daphne decide to take a nap on the floor?" Shaggy wants to know.

"I don't think she's doing this on purpose," Fred concludes. He pats Daphne's cheek to get her to wake up. She does not respond.

Suddenly Scooby's nose twitches.

SNIFF! SNIFF! "Rhut's rat smell?" Scooby asks. His mouth begins to drool. "Rit's dericious!"

SNIFF! SNIFF! "It smells like strawberry shortcake," Shaggy replies. "No, blueberry pie. No, apple pie!"

"This is no time to be thinking about food," Fred scolds. "Daphne needs our help. But — *SNIFF SNIFF* — it sure smells good!"

Turn the page.

A moment later the kids hear a waltz start to play. Men and women dressed in antebellum attire dance in graceful circles around the gang. Beautiful jewelry sparkles in the soft light of hundreds of candles.

"Velma! Look at you! You're a Southern belle!" Fred gasps.

Velma glances down at her outfit. It has transformed from her regular sweater, skirt, and knee socks to a gorgeous gown made of silk.

"Look at yourself, Fred!" Velma giggles.

Fred is dressed in a tailored jacket, waistcoat, and high-waist trousers. His everyday ascot is now silk ruffles.

"Like, I look pretty sharp, too, if I do say so myself," Shaggy grins. He is dressed in formal wear like Fred.

"May I have this dance, *mademoiselle*?" Fred asks as he bows at Velma.

"Why, certainly, *monsieur*," Velma replies as she curtseys.

Fred and Velma join the other dancers in the waltz. Shaggy watches them spin for a few moments, then decides he wants to dance, too.

"Scooby, may I have this dance?" Shaggy asks as he turns to his canine pal.

But Scooby is nowhere to be seen.

"Scooby-Doo, where are you?" Shaggy asks.

"Raggy! Rake up!" Scooby whimpers as he sits next to his unconscious friend. The Mystery Inc. gang is sprawled on the ballroom floor. Their eyes shift in REM sleep.

Scooby doesn't know what has happened. One minute he and the gang smelled a delicious scent, and in the next, everyone fell down, asleep like Daphne.

"Beat it, you meddling mutt!" a harsh voice commands.

Scooby looks toward the sound and sees a ghostly pale man who rushes across the ballroom waving arms as thin as skeleton bones.

"Rit's a rhost!" Scooby gulps in terror.

Turn to page 65.

Scooby-Doo leaps up out of the cook pot and comes down holding a fry pan in one paw to face the fearsome phantom of the kitchen. Scooby's tangle with the pot rack leaves him covered in accidental skillet armor. Suddenly inspired, Scooby strikes a martial arts pose.

"Like, you're Samurai Scooby-Doo!" Shaggy says. He straps on a baking sheet and some pie plates. "It's time for a little Kung Pow action!"

The ghost chef gasps at the sight of Shaggy and Scooby garbed in shiny stainless steel. They look like knights in gleaming armor. Then the ghoul's face turns into a gruesome grimace. Now it's time for Shaggy and Scooby to strike a new pose — frozen in fear!

"Zoinks! We're doomed!" cries Shaggy.

Suddenly Scooby dives back into the gumbo stew pot! He swims a few laps around the edge and then sits inside the vessel as if it's a hot tub.

Turn to page 60.

"Rummy!" Scooby says and gulps down a ladle full of gumbo.

"*Nooo!* You've ruined my recipe!" the ghost protests.

"It tastes good to me," Shaggy says as he slurps a bowl full of Scooby-flavored soup.

"What do you Yankees know of Cajun cuisine? The spices! The sausage! The . . . uh-oh," the ghost stumbles to a halt. "You've figured out who I am."

"You're no ghost," Shaggy proclaims. "You're a real, live chef!"

"Rand a good one, too!" Scooby agrees.

"Really?" the specter sighs. He takes off his spooky mask to reveal a human face. "You're the first ones to say that. The rest of my family doesn't think I have any talent."

Suddenly the rest of Mystery Inc. bursts into the kitchen!

"We heard all the noise and came to investigate," Fred says. "What's going on?"

Scooby and Shaggy take the fake ghost disguise from the chef and secretly plop it into the pot of simmering gumbo as fast as they can.

"Like, we were just sampling a specialty of chef . . . what did you say your name was?" Shaggy as he turns toward the fake phantom.

"Whom are you talking to?" Velma asks. "There's no one in the kitchen except you and Scooby."

"Ruh-roh," Scooby-Doo gulps. "Rit was real!"

"And it was the most delicious adventure ever!" Shaggy says as he slurps down the whole pot of soup.

"Heh-heh-heh! Scooby-Dooby-Stew!" Scooby howls.

THE END

To follow another path, turn to page 11.

Fred and Daphne find themselves face-to-face with a ghastly ghoul! It raises thin, skeletal arms draped in tattered robes. Boney fists grip thick chains that drip with oozing moss.

"*Yaaa!*" Fred and Daphne yell.

"*Bwaaaaah!*" the ghoul shouts back with a gust of icy breath.

Daphne's hair is blasted by the creature's arctic shriek and freezes into icicles. The air around Fred turns to snow and whirls around like a tornado. When it stops, Fred looks like a snowman!

"Oh, no! What happed to my hair?" Daphne asks as her fingers feel all around her head.

The ghoul pulls out a mirror and shows Daphne what she looks like. The ghoul laughs at her. Daphne is not amused. Her face turns red and steam starts to erupt from her ears. Suddenly all the icicles in her hair explode!

Shards of ice fly in every direction. Some shatter against the ghoul. Other pieces shred the snow around Fred and free him.

"Never insult Daphne's hair," Fred says.

The creature gulps and tries to flee, but Daphne stomps on the hem of its ragged robes. "Not so fast, mister," she declares.

"Daphne! What are you doing?" Fred asks.

"If there's one thing I know, it's hair and makeup," Daphne says. "And because of that I know this ghoulish guy is a fake!"

"*Whaaaat?*" Fred and the ghoul gasp at the same time.

Daphne strides around the ghoul and inspects the creature as if it were a fashion model about to walk the runway.

"First, look at this outfit," Daphne demands as she flips the flimsy tatters with her fingers. "Rags? Really? How cliché. And it's not even good fabric. Now look at the makeup. Real ghouls don't wear makeup!"

Turn the page.

"Okay! I'm not a monster, I'm a human," the ghoul confesses. He wipes off his makeup with his sleeve.

"Who are you?" Fred asks.

"My name is Bedford Le Blanc, and I used this ghoul disguise to scare my cousins out of the mansion," the man admits. "We don't get along very well. And my plan was working until you meddling kids showed up! Once you tell my cousins about this, I'm doomed."

"Oh, you're doomed all right — if you don't make a hair appointment for me at Chez Coiffure," Daphne says as she glares at Bedford with furious, fiery eyes.

"Y-yes, ma'am," Bedford agrees sheepishly as he leads them to the way out of the secret passageway.

THE END

To follow another path, turn to page 11.

Scooby stares at the creepy creature coming at him. Then he looks down at Shaggy and the gang lying on the floor. "Ri'll protect rou," Scooby promises his friends.

A surge of courage flows through Scooby's body. He braces all four legs and lets out a brave bark. The ghoulish man stops dead in his tracks.

"Nice doggie," the man says with a smile. He takes a bone out of his pocket and waves it at Scooby.

Scooby looks at the bone and then at the weird man. Scoobs sits back on his haunches and puts his hands on his hips.

"Are rou kidding re?" Scooby-Doo scoffs. "How arout a steak?"

"How about this dog-catcher's net?" The man whips out a giant webbed snare on a pole.

"Ruh-roh," Scooby gulps.

The man swings the net down toward Scooby, but Scooby's legs spin like propellers. He takes off like an airboat on a bayou.

Turn the page.

Scooby escapes the madman's net and runs for his life! It's too bad that the ghoulish guy is supernaturally fast. He chases Scooby around the ballroom. Scooby knows it's up to him to save the gang, but he doesn't have a clue.

"Ri need a ran! What rould Rred do?" Scooby wonders. He tries to think, but that makes him dizzy. "Rokay. Plan B. Reep running!"

Suddenly Scooby runs smack into the ghostly guy. They tumble in a tangle down the length of the ballroom. **CRASH!** They hit the far wall. Scooby sees stars. Then he smells strawberry shortcake.

"*Mmm*, rummy," Scooby sighs as the man squirts a small spray bottle at Scooby, but Scooby doesn't fall asleep like his human friends.

"The dog is immune to my formula!" the man realizes.

"Ri'm not a rog, Ri'm Scooby-Doo!" Scooby declares as he snatches the spray bottle from the man and holds it in front of the guy's face.

"I'm doomed . . ." the man moans.

"You're a hero!" the Mystery Inc. kids proclaim when they finally wake up and see what Scooby-Doo has accomplished. He sits on top of the ghoul who put them into dreamland.

"That canine is smarter than he looks," the man grumbles.

"He was smart enough to stop you — Mr. Redmond LaFleur!" Velma announces. "I recognize you from your portrait in the foyer."

"You meddling kids! You've ruined my scheme!" Redmond complains. "I used my experimental dream formula on my cousins. I wanted the mansion for myself but they wouldn't leave."

"W-where are they?" Shaggy gulps.

"Everyone is upstairs asleep in their beds," Redmond reveals.

"I hope they're dreaming about a waltz," Daphne and Velma sigh.

THE END

To follow another path, turn to page 11.

Shaggy and Scooby make a hasty retreat out of the kitchen, but not before loading their arms full of food.

"After that hair-raising experience, I need something to calm my nerves," Shaggy explains as he gulps down a batch of cupcakes, a rack of barbecued ribs, and a whole apple pie.

"Me, roo," Scooby agrees. He tosses a stack of pulled-pork sandwiches into the air and leaps up to gobble them down.

"Like, I suppose we should look for the rest of the gang and tell them about the ghost," Shaggy says, but Scooby whimpers. "Okay, maybe not. One close encounter was close enough."

As the pals wander down the hall, they hear their friends' voices. They follow the sounds to a room where they see the rest of Mystery Inc. standing around a table. Black candles burn with purple flames and incense curls in smoky ribbons. The scent makes Scooby wrinkle his nose.

"*Achooo!*" Shaggy sneezes. "What's that smell?"

"Ah, two more victims — I mean guests. Come in, come in," says a woman dressed in black. "My name is Delilah. Welcome to my home."

The woman steps around the table toward the pals and waves the incense in their direction. Fred, Daphne, and Velma stare straight ahead and ignore Shaggy and Scooby.

"I see you're enjoying our Southern hospitality," Delilah says and points to the armloads of food Scooby and Shaggy hold.

"Yes, ma'am. Thank you ma'am," Shaggy stammers nervously. He and Scooby automatically curtsey.

"You fellows have manners," Delilah says with a smile. "I like fellows with manners."

Suddenly the woman's eyes seem to spin like hypnotic pinwheels. Shaggy and Scooby can't look anywhere else but at Delilah. Their friends are forgotten. Their snacks are forgotten. All they can see is Delilah. It's as if they have been caught in a spider's web!

Turn to page 75.

Velma jumps in surprise at the sudden sound of the voice. Her hand comes down on the book and pulls it from the shelf. Velma is startled to discover that the book is attached to the shelf by a hinge. A moment later she knows the reason. It's the lever to a secret trapdoor!

Suddenly there is no floor under Velma's feet. The trapdoor opens beneath Velma and she falls into a chute. As she disappears into the darkness, the woman in black stands over the opening and smiles.

"I warned you," the woman says.

"*Yaaaa!*" Velma yells as she slides down, down, down.

At last Velma shoots out of the chute and onto a cold stone floor. A metal grate clangs shut over the chute opening. Velma realizes that she cannot get out the way she got in.

"Where am I?" Velma wonders as she looks at her surroundings.

Turn the page.

Velma soon sees that she is in a room made of stone. The walls, ceiling, and floor are all blocks of granite. In the middle of the chamber rests a huge coffin on a pedestal, also carved from stone. Velma searches all around the room, but she can't find a door.

"Oh, great. I'm trapped in the family crypt," Velma groans. "And if I don't find a way out of here I'm going to end up like whoever's in that coffin."

Velma goes over to the chute opening and yells into the shaft.

"Hello! Is anyone up there? I've fallen down a chute, and I can't get back up!" Velma shouts. There is no reply.

Velma goes back over to the stone coffin and reads the name carved into the side.

"Quinton Lafitte. Well, Mr. Lafitte, it looks like we're going to be spending some time together," Velma sighs.

Turn to page 79.

Daphne backs away from the spinning specter. It howls with an ear-splitting shriek and follows her across the room. Daphne desperately looks for a way out. Suddenly the gleam of a crystal doorknob grabs her attention.

"I don't remember seeing that door when I came in here, but I'm sure glad it's here now!" Daphne declares as she runs toward it.

The ghost wails and chases Daphne as she sprints across the room. She grasps the crystal knob and pulls the door open. As soon as Daphne reaches the next room, she slams the door behind her and leans back against it. Suddenly there is silence.

"Jeepers! I guess I found a phantom menace instead of a phone!" Daphne gasps.

There is no sound coming from the room she just escaped, but Daphne isn't willing to go back and find out why. She looks around the room she's in and sees that it is full of musical instruments.

Turn the page.

A setup for a string quartet is in one corner of the room. A baby grand piano and an antique harpsichord are in the middle of the chamber. A giant pipe organ dominates a whole wall.

"And as usual, there's no phone," Daphne sighs.

Suddenly the pipe organ begins to play as if by invisible hands!

"Jeepers!" Daphne jumps in surprise. Then she laughs at her fear. "Oh, it's probably like one of those self-playing pianos."

The piano and harpsichord suddenly begin to play a waltz all by themselves. Then the string quartet joins in, but no one is playing the instruments!

Daphne runs back to the door. She tugs on the crystal knob, but it's stuck. The shrill sound of a violin makes Daphne turn. Every musical instrument is in the air and flying toward her!

Turn to page 82.

"Hahaha! Welcome to the Widow's Nest! The Black Widow, that is!" Delilah cackles.

"Zoinks! Are you a real spider?" Shaggy asks as the incense starts to cloud his mind and make his body motionless.

"Yuck! I hate spiders!" Delilah yells. "No, I'm a witch who will weave a spell of obedience on you. Your friends are already under my control."

Shaggy swivels his eyes to look over at the rest of the gang standing at attention around the table. Their expressions are blank.

"We're doomed! And I thought the ghost in the kitchen was scary," Shaggy gulps.

"Wait. What ghost in the kitchen?" Delilah asks.

"The one right behind you!" Shaggy says.

As soon as Delilah turns to look behind her, Shaggy and Scooby hit the witch with the food they've had in their arms the whole time. She collapses under the pile of pastries, pies, and barbecue.

Turn the page.

"Fake out!" Shaggy cheers as he and Scooby slap a high five. "Scoobs, you deserve an acting award for your performance."

"Rank rou," Scooby ays and grins. He bows and holds up a candlestick as if it were a trophy.

The pals wave away the hypnotic incense and awaken their friends. Fred, Daphne, and Velma are dazed, but there's no time for Shaggy to explain what happened. The witch starts to come out from under the pile of snacks! The kids flee from the witch's lair. They don't get far. They suddenly face a pack of snarling werewolves!

"Zoinks!" Shaggy gulps. "First, ghosts and witches, now werewolves! We're in a house of horrors!"

"No, we're not. We're in a house of holograms," Velma announces. She points at a projector lens in the ceiling. "My glasses caught the reflection of the beam."

Fred uses his scarf like a slingshot and knocks out the lens with a small makeup case from Daphne's purse. The werewolves disappear.

"Why would someone rig the house with hologram projectors?" Fred wonders.

"Someone wants to make the place look haunted," Velma says.

"You meddling kids!" Delilah yells from behind them.

The unexpected shout makes Shaggy and Scooby jump. Scooby leaps into Shaggy's arms and Shaggy leaps into Fred's arms. The three of them sway like a teetering totem pole.

"I used the projectors to make my reputation as a witch and now you've exposed my secret. I'm ruined!" Delilah confesses.

"You pretended to be something you're not. That's cheating," Fred proclaims.

"Maybe you should switch careers," Velma suggests. "Have you ever considered going into the special effects business?"

THE END

To follow another path, turn to page 11.

The label on the box reads: Quinton Lafitte

Velma sits down on the floor of the crypt and leans her back against the coffin's pedestal. She takes off her glasses and wipes the stone dust from the lenses.

"I've got to find a way out of this creepy crypt. Think, Velma!" Velma tells herself.

Suddenly Velma sees a blur in front of her. She's not wearing her glasses so she has no idea what it is. As soon as Velma puts her glasses back on she wishes she had left them off!

"Jinkies! It's a ghost!" Velma gasps and jumps to her feet.

The ghost floats in the air in front of her. It is as gray as the twilight. After a moment Velma realizes that the ghost is gray because it's dressed in the uniform of a Confederate Army officer.

The ghost bows politely to Velma. She curtseys in response. The ghost smiles and points to the coffin.

"Y-you're Quinton Lafitte!" Velma gasps.

Turn the page.

The ghost bows again to show Velma that she is correct. Then he motions for her to follow him as he floats over to the wall. He points at a small, rough stone in the smooth surface.

"Oh! Is this the way out? Thank you!" Velma says. But when she twists the little stone, she is surprised beyond imagination!

The wall opens to reveal another chamber, but this one doesn't contain a coffin. It's filled with treasure.

"You found it!" a voice shouts from behind Velma. "But it belongs to me! I've been looking for that Civil War fortune for years!"

The woman in black runs into the crypt through a door that wasn't there a moment ago. She shoves Velma out of the way to get at the golden treasure. She lifts up a handful and laughs as she lets it fall around her. Suddenly the gold turns to gray ashes.

Velma is astonished as the wall closes, trapping the woman and the ghost inside. The treasure is lost as soon as it's found.

Velma stumbles back against the stone coffin.

"Hey, Velma! What are you doing down in this creepy old place?" Shaggy asks as he and Scooby wander into the chamber.

"Am I glad to see you guys!" Velma shouts and hugs her friends.

"Whoa! Watch out for the snacks!" Shaggy says as he lifts an armload of sandwiches.

Suddenly the ghost of Quinton Lafitte walks through the wall. Shaggy and Scooby shriek and run! Velma turns to face the spooky specter.

"Um, where's the lady in black?" Velma asks.

The ghost points to the blank wall. The little trigger stone is not visible anymore.

"I get it. She wanted the treasure and now she has it — forever," Velma concludes as a chill goes down her spine. The ghost bows and disappears.

THE END

To follow another path, turn to page 11.

Daphne ducks as a violin smashes against the door right above her head! She finally gets the doorknob to turn, and she escapes back into the adjoining room. She braces herself to face the spinning specter once more.

"Well, this isn't what I was expecting," Daphne admits.

The ghost is gone. So are the old ladies with the crystal ball. For some reason, the room is now decorated in the Art Deco style of the 1920s. An elegant lady dressed in flapper fringes lounges on a couch.

"Hello, dear," the woman says. "Are you here for the party?"

"No, I'm just looking for the phone," Daphne sighs, not expecting to find one.

"Oh, it's just over there," the woman says and points to an old-fashioned telephone on a table.

"Thank you! Our van broke down in front of your house and . . ." Daphne starts to explain. She stops when she tries to pick up the phone and her hand passes right through it.

Turn to page 84.

"Jeepers!" Daphne exclaims. She snatches her hand away from the phone as if it were a cobra.

"You must stay for the party. We're certain to bring the house down!" the woman says.

"N-no thanks," Daphne replies. "I-I'll just find a phone in another room."

Daphne starts to walk toward the door. She doesn't know if it will take her back to the music room or some other place and time. As soon as Daphne takes a step toward the doorway, it stretches away from her. Instead of being ten feet away, now it is twenty feet.

"This place isn't just spooky, it's kooky!" Daphne declares.

As soon as she makes another attempt to cross the room and reach the door, it retreats before her eyes.

"I'll never get out! Every time I look at the door it gets farther away," Daphne realizes. "*Hmm.* What if I just don't look at it?"

Daphne opens her purse and tosses the contents toward the door. A collection of objects lands on the floor in a straight line. Daphne bends to pick up the first item, then the next and the next. She concentrates on retrieving the objects one by one like breadcrumbs and slowly makes her way across the room. Once Daphne has the last item, she shuts her eyes and gropes for the doorknob. She twists the knob.

Daphne falls through the doorway and feels herself slide across marble tiles. When Daphne opens her eyes she sees a handsome man.

"Hello. I'm Redmond LaFleur," he introduces himself. "Welcome to my home."

"Jeepers, you have a strange home, Mr. LaFleur. Especially the west wing," Daphne says.

"You must be mistaken. There is no west wing," Redmond reveals. "It burned down in the 1920s. There was a wild party . . ."

THE END

To follow another path, turn to page 11.

Shaggy and Scooby run out of the haunted kitchen as fast as their frightened feet can carry them. **SCREEEECH!** They come to a dead stop when they hear a shrill scream.

"Like, that's Velma! She's in danger!" Shaggy gasps.

The thought of their friend in trouble is the only thing that makes the pals run toward the sound instead of away from it. They race into the living room. Velma stands in the center of the room with her hands covering her mouth.

"Velma! Are you all right?" Shaggy asks.

Velma does not move a muscle. It's as if she has been frozen. Her eyes are staring at a single spot across the room.

"I'm afraid I might be responsible for your friend's condition," says a gentleman sitting at a desk by the window. He is dressed in modern-day clothing and looks normal, but so far there hasn't been anything normal about this mansion.

Velma's frozen gaze does not move from the man. Her eyes are wide and she breathes with short, panting breaths.

"H-he . . . it-it's . . . y-you . . ." Velma gasps.

"What happened to our friend?" Shaggy asks.

"She saw me," the man replies with a shrug. "I seem to have that effect on people."

Scooby licks Velma with his big tongue. **SLUUUURP!** Velma blinks and snaps out of her daze. She never notices Shaggy or Scooby. She only has eyes for the man at the desk.

"Dan Barley! You're my favorite horror author!" Velma sighs as she gazes at him with an adoring expression on her face.

"Thank you, young lady," Dan replies.

"I was so excited to see you here that I froze," Velma explains, embarrassed. "You write the Vampire Mansion series and, oh my gosh, I just realized that this is the mansion!"

Velma looks as if she is about to faint from the excitement.

Turn the page.

"Zoinks! We're in a vampire mansion?" Shaggy gasps in fear.

Velma finally notices Shaggy and Scooby. She snaps out of her fan fog.

"No, silly. Mr. Barley writes about vampires living in a mansion and uses this house as his inspiration," Velma says.

"Rampires?" Scooby gulps.

"Only in my imagination," Dan says. "But what are you kids doing in my house?"

"We were looking for a phone. Our van broke down. We need to call a tow truck," Velma says.

"Unfortunately, this house has no phone," Dan says. "It is quite cut off from the outside world."

Suddenly there is a crack of thunder and the room goes dark. A ghoulish laugh ripples through the air.

"Jinkies!" Velma yelps.

"Zoinks!" Shaggy shrieks. "Like, why do the lights go out just before the bad stuff happens?"

Turn to page 96.

Velma snatches her hand away from the book as an unexpected voice surprises her. She turns around to see a tall man dressed in black with dark eyes and features as fine as a movie star's. Velma is stunned by his extreme good looks.

"This house is full of hidden . . . secrets," the man reveals as he takes Velma by the elbow and guides her away from the bookcase.

"O-okay," Velma stammers as she lets him take her across the room. For some strange reason her mind is in a fog and she doesn't notice that the man is avoiding the sunlight streaming in through the windows.

"You're a studious-looking young thing. What's your name?" the man asks.

"Velma," Velma replies obediently.

"I'm very pleased to meet you, Velma. My name is Sterling Lafitte," the man says and kisses her hand. His lips are cold on her skin, but Velma feels a rush of warmth speed up her arm to her brain.

Turn the page.

"How charming!" Sterling chuckles when he sees Velma blush. "I haven't encountered anyone like you in ages."

Sterling leans closer to Velma. All she can see is his hypnotizing eyes. They seem to lock her in place. She can't think or move, not even when he smiles and reveals sharp white fangs! Sterling licks his lips and bends toward Velma's neck.

"Hey! There you are!" a voice interrupts.

Sterling jumps back from Velma and pretends to straighten his tie. Shaggy and Scooby amble into the room. Their arms are full of snacks.

"Like, we found the kitchen, but we didn't find a phone," Shaggy says.

"Rut re found food!" Scooby-Doo declares. He tosses a stack of sandwiches into the air and lets them fall into his mouth. "Rummy!"

"Like, who's your friend, Velma?" Shaggy asks as he grins at Sterling.

The man is not happy about the interruption. He snarls at the two pals, showing his fangs.

"Zoinks! It's a vampire! Run!" Shaggy shrieks.

Scooby and Shaggy spin their legs at turbo-speed and take off, leaving a cloud of dust. The vampire coughs and waves away the dust with his hand. When it clears, he sees that Velma has not moved. He smiles and reaches for her.

"Like, keep your fangs to yourself!" Shaggy shouts as he snatches Velma from the vampire. He lifts Velma onto his shoulder and runs back out of the room as fast as he can go.

As soon as Velma is beyond Sterling's hypnotizing gaze she comes to her senses. She is surprised to find herself draped over Shaggy's shoulder!

"Shaggy! What's going on? Put me down!" Velma says.

"Rit's a rampire!" Scooby replies as he frantically points behind them.

"Don't be ridiculous. There is no such thing as a —" Velma starts to say and then sees the fanged fiend racing toward them. "Never mind! Run!"

Turn to page 99.

The furious phantom swirls around the room like a white tornado. Daphne tries to flee but the vortex rolls over her. She feels the air being sucked from her lungs. Her feet lift off the floor.

Suddenly the door to the room opens. Shaggy, Scooby, and the rest of the Mystery Inc. gang take two steps into the room and then freeze at the sight in front of their eyes!

"Zoinks! There's a hurricane in the house!" Shaggy yelps.

The tornado stops as if a switch has been flipped. The vortex collapses. Daphne lands on her feet, but now a thick goo covers her from head to foot. She staggers under the weight of the slimy mess.

"Vuba . . . Frub . . . Shoooooby," Daphne tries to say their names with a mouthful of gunk. She lumbers toward her friends, looking for help.

"*Yaaaa!*" they shriek and get ready to run. "It's a monster! It's a ghost!"

"It's food!" Scooby says as he inhales a delicious scent.

Turn to page 94.

Scooby-Doo leaps toward the thing his pals think is a gooey ghoul. Then he licks it!

"Ewww, Scoobs!" Shaggy squirms at the sight.

"Rit's rummy!" Scooby declares.

"It's me!" Daphne groans as she wipes off the goop.

"That is not a good look on you," Velma says.

"Like, Scooby's right. This is pretty tasty!" Shaggy says as he slurps a sample.

"What is it?" Fred asks.

Shaggy and Scooby see hearts float in front of their eyes. They are in love with what they've tasted.

"Cheese!" they shout.

Suddenly the pals become another type of tornado as they whirl around Daphne and lap up every speck of gooey cheese from her head to her feet. They collapse on the floor with bulging bellies and smiles on their faces.

"*Buurrrrp!*" Scooby belches.

"Good one, buddy. *Sniff!* Ahhh. That's a classic French Brie," Shaggy proclaims.

"Wait, you can identify the cheese?" Velma gasps.

"Sure! Scoobs and I aren't gourmets, but we know our food!" Shaggy replies.

"There's a mystery in this mansion!" Daphne exclaims.

"It sure tastes great!" Shaggy declares.

"There might be more where that cheese came from, if we can find it," Fred suggests.

Scooby puts his nose to the ground and sniffs like a bloodhound. Shaggy gets on his hands and knees and does the same as Scooby. The pals strike a pointing pose like a pair of hunting dogs.

"Riss Reese!" Scooby announces.

"Parmesan!" Shaggy says. He and Scooby race out of the room. The gang follows.

"It won't be much of a mystery if they lead us to the kitchen," Velma says.

Turn to page 103.

Shaggy, Scooby, and Velma grope around in the dark. "This is worse than losing my glasses," Velma mutters.

Shaggy sees a pale shape across the room. He walks over to the shape, but when he goes to touch it his hand goes right through it!

"*Yaaaa!* A ghost!" Shaggy yells.

"Calm down, Shaggy. That's no ghost, it's a 3-D image," Velma explains.

"Oh, sure. Like, I knew that," Shaggy says. "But where is it coming from?"

"Rover rere," Scooby says as he waves his paw in front of a beam. The image disappears and reappears.

Velma finally finds a candle and lights it. Now she and her pals can see that the beam is coming from a small hole in a painting. When Velma moves the painting to look behind it, a door opens in the wall.

"I see stairs," Velma says. "Let's see where they go."

Shaggy and Scooby follow Velma down the stairs. The steps spiral down and end at a large metal door.

"It looks like the door on a bank vault," Velma says.

"Like, why would someone have a vault under their house?" Shaggy wonders.

"Reasure!" Scooby exclaims.

Immediately Scooby and Shaggy try to open the door. They grab the giant tumbler and struggle to spin it. The door swings open and the friends gasp at what they see inside. Pale figures rise and stumble toward them!

"Zoinks! Ghosts! This isn't a treasure vault, it's the family crypt!" Shaggy screams.

"Those aren't ghosts, they're living people!" Velma realizes. "I recognize one of them from the 3-D image upstairs."

"My name is Quincy Lafitte and these are my cousins. You kids saved our lives!" the man says.

Turn the page.

"Like, glad to help out, but why were you locked in that gloomy tomb?" Shaggy asks.

"Cousin Dan did it!" one of the others replies. "He wants the mansion to promote his books!"

"And I would have gotten away with it if it hadn't been for you meddling kids!" a voice declares from behind them.

"Mr. Barley!" Velma gasps.

"I tried to scare you away with the 3-D image, but you were too curious," Dan grumbles.

"It's a good thing, too. They followed the clues and saved us," Quincy says.

As everyone goes back upstairs, Velma looks depressed. "What's wrong, Velma? We caught the bad guy," Shaggy says.

"But the bad guy turned out to be my favorite author." Velma sighs. "Now that's a real horror story."

THE END

To follow another path, turn to page II.

Shaggy, Scooby, and Velma run down the hallway. They go around a corner at top speed and smack into Fred and Daphne!

"Whoa! What's the hurry, guys?" Fred asks.

"R-rampire!" Scooby stammers.

"Don't be ridiculous. There's no such thing as —" Fred starts to say.

Lafitte comes around the corner and confronts the gang with glaring eyes and fearsome fangs.

"Never mind! Run!" Fred shouts.

Shaggy and Scooby lead the pack to the only place in the mansion they feel safe — the kitchen!

"Quick! Our only hope is to hide in plain sight. Everybody, put on these chef's clothes," Fred says as he hands the gang white kitchen uniforms and puffy chef's hats.

When the vampire Lafitte bursts into the kitchen, he only sees cooks at work, not the kids. Lafitte is frustrated as he looks around the room but can't find his prey.

Turn the page.

"I've got a plan to get rid of this guy," Fred whispers to Velma and Daphne. As soon as he tells them his scheme, they put it into action.

"*Monsieur!* Welcome to *moi* kitchen! You must be hungry," Fred says as he guides Sterling Lafitte to a table. Velma and Daphne spread a tablecloth and place silverware in a flurry.

"I've been thirsting for a good meal," Lafitte says as he sits down.

"Chef! Chef!" Fred commands. He claps his hands and Chef Shaggy and Chef Scooby run to the table with plates piled high with garlic bread.

"*La* first course," Fred proclaims. The vampire eats all the garlic bread and looks at Chef Fred, expecting the next course.

"Chef! Chef! *La* spaghetti!" Fred shouts.

Shaggy and Scooby present a plate heaped high with spaghetti and sauce. Scooby sprinkles extra cheese and garlic over the dish. Sterling slurps up the garlic noodles.

"Ah-ha! *La* fake!" Fred declares.

Turn to page 102.

Scooby-Doo uses a spaghetti noodle like a lasso and pulls out Lafitte's fake vampire fangs.

"Real vampires don't eat garlic," Fred proclaims.

"You meddling kids!" Lafitte complains. "You've ruined my perfect scheme."

"Let me guess," Velma says. "You wanted the family mansion for yourself."

"Or you were searching for a family treasure," Daphne suggests.

"Rut about an old ramily recipe?" Scooby drools.

"No! I pretended to haunt the house as a vampire because I wanted a reality show," Sterling confesses. "I was going to call it *Vampire Mansion*."

"Personally, I'd prefer the show to be called *Mystery Incorporated*!" Fred says.

THE END

To follow another path, turn to page 11.

The gang hurries after the sniffing sleuths. They halt in front of a trio of portraits.

"Those are the three old ladies I saw," Daphne says. "Violet, Daisy, and Rose LaFleur. How did Shaggy and Scooby know?"

"Like, we didn't. The trail leads to this spot," Shaggy shrugs.

"Then we've reached a dead end," Velma says.

"Maybe not. I have a theory," Fred declares. He runs his hands around the paintings. Suddenly the wall swings inward like a door.

"A secret passage!" Daphne says.

Shaggy and Scooby eye the dark opening with suspicion, but the scent of cheese beckons. They lead the way into the gloomy passageway.

The gang walks along the dim corridor until they come to a stone staircase. The steps go downward, deeper under the mansion.

"*Hmm*, homes of this era usually don't have basements," Velma states. "This is probably the family crypt."

Turn the page.

"C-c-crypt?" Shaggy stammers. "You mean a tomb . . . like in Dracula?"

Scooby whimpers and hugs his pal.

"The only vampires in New Orleans are in novels," Velma says. She starts to go down the stairs. "Come on, let's see what's down there."

Shaggy and Scooby reluctantly follow the rest of Mystery Inc. down the cold stone steps. The scent of cheese is forgotten.

But when the kids reach the bottom of the stairs, they gasp at what they see!

"Cheese!" Shaggy sighs in rapture.

The large chamber in front of them is filled with shelves and shelves of golden wheels of goodness. Shaggy and Scooby race toward the nearest stack.

Suddenly a hideous figure in white blocks their path!

"*Yaaa!* A cheese ghost!" Shaggy shouts in alarm.

"Rat's no rhost. Rat's reese," Scooby says as he sniffs the scented spirit. Suddenly he takes a long lick from head to toe. "Rummy!"

"Scooby's right! That's no ghost, that's Rose LaFleur! I recognize her from the portrait upstairs!" Daphne exclaims.

"I'm Rose's great granddaughter, Primrose," the false ghost confesses. "I was using the secret basement to store illegal cheese."

"Illegal cheese? That's a new one, even for us," Velma says.

"It's worth millions, and I would have gotten away with it except for you meddling kids," Primrose grumbles.

"Rillions?" Scooby says as he and Shaggy drool and gaze at the stacked wheels of cheese.

"That's too rich for my tastes. Cheese is off the menu for us, Scoobs." Shaggy sighs.

THE END

To follow another path, turn to page II.

AUTHOR

Laurie S. Sutton has read comics since she was a kid. She grew up to become an editor for Marvel, DC Comics, Starblaze, and Tekno Comics. She has written Adam Strange for DC, Star Trek: Voyager for Marvel, plus Star Trek: Deep Space Nine and Witch Hunter for Malibu Comics. There are long boxes of comics in her closet where there should be clothing and shoes. Laurie has lived all over the world. She currently resides in Florida.

ILLUSTRATOR

Scott Neely has been a professional illustrator and designer for many years. Since 1999, he's been an official Scooby-Doo and Cartoon Network artist, working on such licensed properties as Dexter's Laboratory, Johnny Bravo, Courage the Cowardly Dog, Powerpuff Girls, and more. He has also worked on Pokémon, Mickey Mouse Clubhouse, My Friends Tigger & Pooh, Handy Manny, Strawberry Shortcake, Bratz, and many other popular characters. He lives in a suburb of Philadelphia and has a scrappy Yorkshire Terrier, Alfie.

GLOSSARY

antebellum (AN-tee-BEL-uhm)—existing before the American Civil War

architecture (AR-ki-tek-chur)—the style in which buildings are designed

bayou (BYE-oo)—a stream that runs slowly through a swamp and leads to or from a lake or river

crypt (KRIPT)—an underground chamber for burial

hologram (HOL-uh-gram)—a three-dimensional picture made by laser beams

hypnotic (hip-NOT-ik)—tending to cause sleep

incense (IN-senss)—a substance that is burned to give off a sweet smell

investigate (in-VESS-tuh-gate)—to search and examine in detail

occupant (OK-yuh-puhnt)—a person who uses space in a certain place or area

optical illusion (OP-tuh-kuhl i-LOO-zhuhn)—something that you think you see that is not there

sarcophagus (sahr-KOF-uh-guhs)—a stone coffin

specter (SPEK-tur)—a ghost

trompe l'oeil (TRAWM-PEH-LEE)—a style of painting that uses realistic images to create optical illusions

How did Scooby-Doo escape the haunted house?

a. He played on the run-down piano until he found the right key!

b. He unlocked the door with a spoo-key!

c. He pretended to be a used candle and went out!

What kind of dancing do vampires like?

a. The fangdango!

b. They love getting into the valtz!

c. Anything that's neck to neck!

Where do baby vampires go during the day?

a. The day-scare center.

b. They take a coffin break.

c. They go a little batty!

What color do ghosts paint their house?
a. Navy boo!
b. Yello-o-o-o-o-o-o-o-o-o-o-o-o-!
c. Gang-**GREEN!**

Why do witches like wearing name tags?
a. So they can tell witch is witch.
b. All those broom mates are confusing!
c. They like writing out their names, since they're so good at spelling!

Where did Scooby find the haunted house?
a. On a dead end.
b. Next to the ghost office!
c. In Tombstone, Arizona!

What does Shaggy call a nervous witch?
a. A twitch!
b. A worrywart!
c. Sorcer-restless!